# The Abominable Snowman

For Mum, Dad,
Liam and Suzanne
— F. P.

To Giacomo
and Rebecca
— S. F.

Barefoot Books
2067 Massachusetts Ave
Cambridge, MA 02140

Series Editor: Gina Nuttall
Text copyright © 2011 by Fran Parnell
Illustrations copyright © 2003 & 2011 by Sophie Fatus
The moral rights of Fran Parnell and Sophie Fatus have been asserted

First published in the United States of America by Barefoot Books, Inc in 2011
This story is an abridged version of a chapter of
*The Barefoot Book of Monsters*, published in 2003

Graphic design by Helen Chapman, West Yorkshire, UK
Reproduction by B&P International, Hong Kong
Printed in China on 100% acid-free paper by Printplus, Ltd
This book was typeset in Chalkduster, Gilligan's Island and Sassoon Primary
The illustrations were prepared in acrylics

Sources:
Sharma, Nagendra. *Folk Tales of Nepal*. Sterling Publishers Pvt, Ltd., 1976.

Vaidya, Karuna Kar, editor. *Folk Tales of Nepal*. Ratna Pustak Bhandar, 1971.

ISBN 978-1-84686-558-9

Library of Congress Cataloging-in-Publication Data is available under
LCCN 2011002938

1 3 5 7 9 8 6 4 2

# The Abominable Snowman

## A Story from Nepal

Retold by Fran Parnell • Illustrated by Sophie Fatus

**Barefoot Books**
step inside a story

# Contents

# CHAPTER 1

# The Very Lazy Boy

Long ago and far away, there lived a poor woman and her son, Ramay. They lived in a small hut high in the mountains.

Ramay was a kind boy and his mother loved him very much. But Ramay was lazy. In fact, he was very, VERY lazy.

He just sat outside all day
doing nothing. Hour after hour,
he watched the birds flying and
the clouds floating by.

You are so
lazy, Ramay!

His mother asked him to collect wood for the fire. But Ramay just sat, so the fire died out. His mother asked him to sweep the floor. But Ramay just sat, so the dust got thicker so thicker.

Will you sweep the floor?

One day Ramay's mother lost her temper. She was angry. "Lazybones!" she shouted at him.

"You are lazy and good for nothing! Get out of this house. Don't come back until you have done some honest work!" She chased him out of the hut and slammed the door behind him. BANG!

Ramay was very surprised.
He did not understand why his
mother was so angry. He walked
off into the mountains, wondering
what to do. He walked and
thought. He thought and walked.

Soon Ramay was
a long, long way from home.
He was worried. He knew that
evening was coming. It would
soon be dark.

# CHAPTER 2

# The Hidden Cave

Ramay's tummy rumbled like thunder. He realized that he was very hungry. "Maybe there is something to eat in my pocket," he said to himself.

He put his hand into his
pocket and scratched about.
What luck! He found three
bits of stale bread.

He sat down among the
twisted roots of an old tree
and got comfortable.

I'm very
hungry.

While he prepared to eat his simple
meal, Ramay chattered to himself about
the crumbs of bread.

"Hmmm," he said. "Should I just eat
one now and save the other two for later?
Or should I gobble up all three at once?"

Now, Ramay did not know it, but
there was something hidden beneath him.
Under the roots of the tree where he sat
was a cave. In the cave lived a Shokpa
with his wife and their baby.

A Shokpa is a magical mountain creature. It is also called an "abominable snowman." "Abominable" means horrible.

A Shokpa's hair is as thick
as a bear's to keep out the cold.
And It Is as whIte as the snow to
help him hide. So a Shokpa looks
like a horrible snowman.

The Shokpa heard Ramay
talking and began to tremble
with fear. "A terrible monster
is standing over our cave," the
Shokpa said to his wife.

"I heard him talking. He is going to eat us. He is trying to decide whether to eat us up one at a time or eat us all together!"

The Shokpa's wife clutched her child tightly to her hairy chest. The frightened family huddled together. Their sharp teeth chattered and their bony knees clattered together like drumsticks.

"O terrible monster!" called the Shokpa. "Please, PLEASE, do not eat my family. I beg you! We are very hairy and very thin. We are not very tasty at all. Promise not to eat us and I will give you my magic wand. It will give you whatever you wish for."

Go and eat something else.

# CHAPTER 3

# The Magic WaNd

The Shokpa's voice boomed up from below. It made Ramay leap to his feet. Ramay was amazed, but he wasn't afraid. He realized that the creature below was afraid of him! The Shokpa thought that Ramay was the monster!

So Ramay decided to play a
trick. In a gruff and growly voice he
boomed back.

"Well, I suppose I could use your wand as a toothpick. I have just had a bite to eat. I think that one of the goats I ate is stuck in my back teeth!"

As soon as he had spoken, a wand appeared out of the ground in front of him. Ramay snatched it up in delight. Then he set off home to show his mother.

But the sun began to set behind the mountains. Ramay had only traveled a short distance and he was still a long way from home. He knew that he had to find somewhere to stay for the night.

Ramay looked here and he looked there for shelter. Just as he was about to give up, he spotted a little shack through the trees.

He ran to the shack and knocked on the door. An old woodcutter answered and invited Ramay in.

Ramay was so
excited about his
adventure that he told
the whole story to the
man. He told him all
about the magic wand.

"Test it out now just to make sure it really works!" said the old man. He had a wicked gleam in his eye, but Ramay did not see it. So Ramay wished for a meal for the two of them.

Before they could blink, a
delicious feast appeared. There was
juicy pork and soft noodles, roast
chicken, spicy lentils, ripe fruits and
a big bowl of sweet molasses.

Soon the old man and Ramay
had eaten all they could. Then,
before they could blink, the empty
dishes disappeared again.

Ramay curled up on
the floor and fell fast
asleep. His tummy was
full of food and his head
was full of happy dreams.

30

# CHAPTER 4

# The Rotten Trickster

The next morning, Ramay thanked the old woodcutter for letting him sleep in the shack. Then he picked up the wand and left. He was feeling very happy. He hopped and skipped and sang all the way home.

"Look, Mother!" he cried, as he ran into their little hut. "An abominable snowman gave me his magic wand. It grants wishes. It will give us everything we want! We will never be poor again."

"Abominable snowman?
Magic wand?" repeated Ramay's
mother. She could not believe it.
"What nonsense! You are such a
daydreamer, Ramay."

"It's true," argued Ramay. "Just
watch this! O magic wand, please
give my mother a bag of golden
coins." But nothing happened.

The sly old woodcutter had
taken the wand for himself.
That was why he had a wicked
gleam in his eye. He had put a
plain stick in its place.

Ramay shook the stick.
He tapped it on the table.
He waved it wildly around
his head. But still no gold
appeared.

"You silly, SILLY boy!"
shouted his mother. She did not
know whether to laugh or to cry.

You are such
a fool!

"Throw away that stupid
bit of wood and make yourself
useful. Fetch some water from the
well for me."

But Ramay was already
out of the door. He raced
back to the Shokpa's cave.
He was sure that it was the
monster who had tricked him.

When he reached the old tree, he shouted at the roots. "Shokpa! This time, I am going to eat your whole family for breakfast. You are a rotten trickster!"

The poor Shokpa did not know what Ramay was talking about. He asked Ramay to explain.

When the Shokpa had heard Ramay's tale, he said, "O terrible monster, I did not trick you. It must have been the old woodcutter.

But I didn't trick you!

"Take my wife's magic wand. Command it to beat anyone who touches it without your permission. Then go and stay again in the old man's shack. See what happens."

# The Beaten Trickster

Yippee! A new wand.

A second wand appeared from out of the ground. Ramay picked it up and did what the abominable snowman suggested. First, he commanded the wand to beat anyone who touched it without his permission.

Then he went back to the
woodcutter's shack. He used the
second wand to wish for another feast
for himself and the old man. And what
a feast it was! After they had eaten,
Ramay fell fast asleep.

In the middle of the night,
Ramay was woken up by the
most terrible noise.

Ouch!

There was crashing furniture,
a strange thumping sound and
loud cries for help. The second
wand was chasing the old
woodcutter around and around
the shack.

The old man was shouting
out at the top of his voice. "Help,
HELP! Tell it to stop!" he yelled.
He tried to get out of the way of
the flying stick.

Hi Mom, I'm home!

Ramay felt a bit sorry for the old man. "STOP!" he told the wand. Then the terrified woodcutter admitted that he had stolen the first wand.

He apologized a thousand times
and returned the first wand to Ramay.
Immediately Ramay wished for the
second wand to fly back to the Shokpa's
wife. Then he returned home with the
first magic wand.

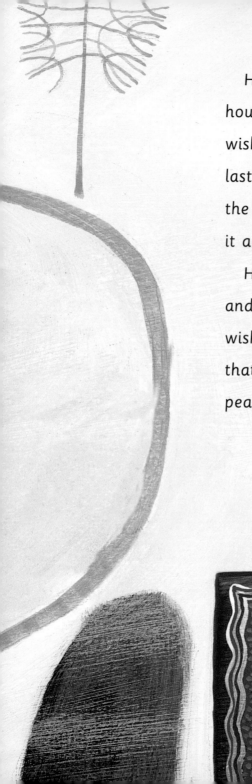

He wished for a fine new house and it appeared. He wished for enough gold to last him and his mother the rest of their lives. And it appeared.

His mother was amazed and delighted. All their wishes were granted. From that day on, they lived in peace and had plenty.

And Ramay did not forget
the Shopka and his family.
He also made a few secret
wishes for them.

"May your cave be snug and dry," he whispered. "May your tummies be always full.

"May your fur always keep you warm. And may the three of you never be eaten by monsters!"